P9-AGK-736

*

LIFE:

An Eternal Hymn

BY

J.J. BHATT

1

All rights reserved. No part of this publication is
reproduce, stored in a retrieval system for transmitted
in a form or any means electronic, mechanical, photo-
copying recording, or without the permission of the
copyright holder.

ISBN:

9798861679664

Title:

LIFE: *An*
Eternal Hymn

Author:

J.J. Bhatt

Published and Distributed by Amazon and
Kindle worldwide.

This book is manufactured in the Unites States of America

Recent Books by J.J. Bhatt

HUMAN ENDEAVOR: Essence & Mission/ A Call for Global Awakening, (2011)

ROLLING SPIRITS: *Being Becoming* /A Trilogy, (2012)

ODYSSEY OF THE DAMNED: *A Revolving Destiny,* (2013).

PARISHRAM: Journey of the Human Spirits, (2014).

TRIUMPH OF THE BOLD: *A Poetic Reality,* (2015).

THEATER OF WISDOM , *(2016).*

MAGNIFICENT QUEST: *Life, Death & Eternity,* (2016).

ESSENCE OF INDIA: A Comprehensive Perspective, (2016).

ESSENCE OF CHINA: *Challenges & Possibilities,* (2016).

BEING & MORAL PERSUASION: *A Bolt of Inspiration,* (2017).

REFELCTIONS, RECOLLECTIONS & EXPRESSIONS, (2018).

ONE, TWO, THREE... ETERNITY: *A Poetic Odyssey, (*2018).

INDIA: Journey of Enlightenment, (2019a).

SPINNING MIND, SPINNING TIME: *C'est la vie,* (2019b).Book 1.

MEDITATION ON HOLY TRINITY, *(2019c), Book 2.*

ENLIGHTENMENT: *Fiat lux,* (2019d), Book 3.

BEING IN THE CONTEXTUAL ORBIT: *Rhythm, Melody & Meaning, (*2019e).

QUINTESSENCE: *Thought & Action,* (2019f).

THE WILL TO ASCENT: *Power of Boldness & Genius,* (2019g).

RIDE ON A SPINNING WHEEL: *Existence Introspected, (*2020a).

A FLASH OF LIGHT: Splendors, Perplexities & Riddles, (2020b).

ON A ZIG ZAG TRAIL: *The Flow of Life,* (2020c).

3

UNBOUNDED: An Inner Sense of Destiny (2020d).

REVERBERATIONS: The *Cosmic Pulse,* (2020e).

LIGHT & DARK: *Dialogue and Meaning,* (2021a).

ROLLING REALITY: Being in flux, (2021b).

FORMAL SPLENDOR: *The Inner Rigor,* (2021c).

TEMPORAL TO ETERNAL: *Unknown Expedition,* (2021d).

TRAILBLAZERS: *Spears of Courage,* (2021e).

TRIALS & ERRORS: A Path to Human Understanding, (2021f).

MEASURE OF HUMAN EXPERIENCE: *Brief Notes,* (2021g).

LIFE: An Ellipsis (2022a).

VALIDATION: The Inner Realm of Essence (2022b).

LET'S ROLL: *Brave Heart,* (2022c). / DISCOURSE: *Being & Mission* (2022d).

BEING BECOMING, (2022 e) . / Essential Humanity: a Conceptual Clarity

(2022f) / INVINCIBLE, (2022g)/ THE CODE: *DESTINY,* (2022h).

LIFE DIMYSTIFIED, (2022i) / ESSENTIAL HUMANITY, (2022h).

EPHEMERAL SPLENDOR, (2023a) / CHAOTIC *HARMONY,* (2023b).

INTELLECTUAL MYSTICISM, (2023C).

WILL TO BELIEVE (2023D).

EXPECTATIONS & REALITY, (2023E).

THREAD THAT BINDS, (2023F).

ONCE & FOREVER, (2023G).

PERPLEXED, (2023H)

GO BEYOND (2023i) / BEING & JOURNEY (2023j

LIFE: *AN ETERNAL HYMN* (2023k.

Preface

LIFE: *An Eternal Hymn,* what an amazing reverberation that keeps human spirit incessantly exploring, "What is it all about?" Let life be a logical necessity of "Self Truth connecting it with all that is".

In the big picture, let life per se be an eternal hymn of every human soul wanting to be an enlightened experience. In the final analysis, the awakened minds must dismiss the notion about life, "The more it changes, the more it is the same, *plus ca change!"*

J.J. Bhatt

Contents

Life

Only in
Uncertainty,
We keep
Exploring

Only through
Struggles,
We keep
Ascending

That be
The power
Pushing us

To unveil
Truth of the
Mind itself

Let it roll
Forward, and
Let us be free

From
False assumptions
And all historic
Blunders and sins…

Copyright © 2023 by J.J. Bhatt

Rejuvenation

We the
Sentient, what if
We are lost between
Known and the unknown
Forever

It's a weird
Feeling. It's like
Falling off the ramp and
Never returning to the
Main path

Well, that's been
The state of the very
Old mind

Let it
All be dropped from
The subjective beliefs
And the pseudo-claims

Let the new
Mind restart; walking
Along a right trail and
Be the illumined soul
Forever…

Copyright © 2023 by J.J. Bhatt

Reckoning

Don't push
Him too hard,
To know the
Unknown in such
A hurry

Don't rush
This human to be
Vanished from the
Earth so soon

Let him
Live long enough
To understand,
"Who he is and what
He ought to be"

Don't push
Him off the track
Don't kicking him off
The right path

Let him
Keep rolling through
Light and dark, and
Let him grasp, "He's
For a worthy cause…"

Copyright © 2023 by J.J. Bhatt

Mirage

Every "I" is
The glowing inspiration;
Marching through the
The Anthrocosmic
Link

Yes, every "I"
Is a determined soul;
Reaching where "All
Meanings clarify,
In an instant"

That is the
Beginning, transition and
Ultimate return to the
Source

Oh yes,
Every "I" is
A live universe
Dancing through eternity
As his/her final reward…

Copyright © 2023 by J.J. Bhatt

Being &
Time

Once he was
An innocent child
Who wondered
With big eyes, and
Believing all that
What he heard

Once he was
A mischievous teen
Who kept fighting for
His identity & pride

Once he turned a
Grown man, his attitude
Changed as he ran after
Wealth, power and fame

Well,
As a corrupted man,
He played many games
And of course, profited
Well in the end

Now in
His Sun set, the
Man is reduced to
Nothingness; fighting for
His old sins and loneliness…

Copyright © 2023 by J.J. Bhatt

Power of Love

Love,
What a mesmerizing
Feelings to be swept
Away from
The troubled world

That is
You Dear Heart
That is
Your sweet smile and
Deep affection and care

Love, love and
Love everywhere in
In my every thought
You are the reality of
My perfect dream

So dear Love,
Yes my sweet heart,
Our journey is "Forever"
Since the first kiss

Let us
Just keep rolling
From here to eternity
Being one blended Soul…

Copyright © 2023 by J.J. Bhatt

Celebration

Life is the
Real celebration,
It's the only constant
Rhythm of all dreams

Life is
The beginning and
The end, but always
A new beginning

Let it
Be the trust of
Of every man,
Woman and child

Let it
Be the determination
Of every struggling
Being

Let it
Be the challenge
To win the game in
The end…

Copyright © 2023 by J.J. Bhatt

Base Reference

Let
There be
Enlightened
Beings; leading
The world toward
Peace and

Let
There be humans
With new attitude
To remove
Many obstacles,

And let them
Pave the path toward
Harmony and hope

So we can
Deeply appreciate
The value of humanity
In our time…

Copyright © 2023 by J.J. Bhatt

Time

Time to
Explore all the
Unknowns before
We're off the edge

Time to
Redefine our own
Being to meet the
Highest noble goal

Time to
Take a bold stand
And never quit the
Challenge
From the scene

Time to
Wake-up from the
Deep slumber, and
Take charge for time
Is of the essence...

Copyright © 2023 by J.J. Bhatt

Being & Meaning

Every war
Is a failure of the
Intelligent mind

Every violent
Act is the insult to
Our common sense

And, every
Falsity peddled in the
Godly name must be
Questioned critically

Let the
World relearn to
Worship, "How to
Relate positively with
His lost children?"

Copyright © 2023 by J.J. Bhatt

Participants

The golden mean
Must be the norm than
Exception

Let it
Be the beginning of
Our collective journey
From this point on

Let humans
Restore order from
The historic disorder

Let them
Face the challenges
Of today and

Boldly resolve
Them for the future
Of the generations to
Follow

Let humanity
Transform from hubris
And gluttony of greed
And, let it strengthen the
Moral fabrics before it's
Too late…

Copyright © 2023 by J.J. Bhatt

Big
Question

Everything
My be subject to
Change, but the human
Nature remain a big
Question

There once
Were the cave dwellers
Later turned hunters,
Then farmers, warriors
And ruthless rulers

Of course,
All along superstitions,
Myths and even organized
Religions kept the believers
Under their grips

Well, once
The industrial men came
On the scene... the world
Came under their spell of
Few greedy powerful

Today, this
Ongoing consumerism,
Globalization and the
Exploding hi-tech seems
To have hijacked the
Original humans!

Copyright © 2023 by J.J. Bhatt

Endeavor

We're
All victims of
Our romantic illusion

Often,
Lost in the state of
Very high ambition

While ignoring,
"What is our
Reality
In this turbulent
World"

Again,
In this mentally
Conceptualized
Divinely obsession

We've been
Thrown off the track;
Neglecting our very
Ethical responsibility

Time to
Gather –up our
Collective strength and
Get busy
To build the world of
"Peace, Progress and
Harmony; inspiring
The young."

Copyright © 2023 by J.J. Bhatt

Reflections

Often,
In the milieu of
Ignorance and
Excessive narcissistic
Attitude

We blend
Facts and fancies;
Consequently we're
Thrown off the real
Path

That essentially
Seems
To be the patterns
Of human history

Time to
Eviscerate the old
Habits and

Time to move
On toward a
"Meaningful
Community of the
Awakened Souls…"

Copyright © 2023 by J.J. Bhatt

Uncertainty
Rules

What if
"Truth" what we
Seek may not be the
Same as that of

Super-
Intelligent aliens
Elsewhere in this
Mighty Universe?

And, what if the
Notion of "God "
What we hold may
Not be the same as
Well?

If all
Reality is nothing,
But a subjective
Interpretation?

Perhaps,
Uncertainty rules
The magic mind either
Here or out over there
In this
Magnifique Universe?

Copyright © 2023 by J.J. Bhatt

First Step

To be
The genuine inheritor
Of the moral fortitude,
Vital to know the basic
Rules

To brush off
All negative thoughts,
Words and stay focus with
The noble goal

To learn,
"How to maintain
Trust and confidence
Of others in you"

Yes, always
Listen what others got
To say in the matter

Take a fearless
Stand, if injustice is
Blatant before the world

Never quit,
When fighting against
Any irrational belief
That is detrimental to
Harmony and peace of
The whole…

Copyright © 2023 by J.J. Bhatt

Being & Freedom

Life is a
Journey of exploring,
Experiencing, imagining,
And awakening

So make
The best out of it while
Walking through it every
Minute

Don't fall
To the trivial things:
False beliefs, pseudo-
Claims by the zealots,
Or the double-talks of
The guardians

Be smart,
Be awake and know
The trail well where
Real meaning yet to
Be unveiled

Learn
To live in simplicity
And with a strong
Disciplined thoughts,
Words and good deeds,
And be free at last…

Copyright © 2023 by J.J. Bhatt

Reality
As Is

Humanity,
What a blend of
Moral and melodramatic
Experience!

That must
Be the "Give and take"
Of our dreams, wishes and
Creative wants

That got
To be the ebb and flow
Of the journey we've been
On for a long

Life seems
Great and fulfilling,
So long you walk along

With
Your right vision,
Moral intention, and
The rational insight

Life,
Silently asking,
"To get up and walk
Toward the path
Of perfection as far as
You can…"

Copyright © 2023 by J.J. Bhatt

Noble
Mission

Let it be
Known by all the
Struggling mortals,

"We're
The continuum
Force of the past; heading
Toward a future that's not
So clear to us"

In-between,
There is a narrow strip
Called, "the Present"
What we're the ephemeral
Owners of life

We're, in fact
On a borrowed time
And the journey to reach
"Self-Truth" seems so far
And beyond

Let us
Change the direction;
By changing our human nature
To build a world of sanity,
Harmony and true humanity
Before our times up…

Copyright © 2023 by J.J. Bhatt

The
Source

Let there
Be Light,
Let there
Be Hope and
Let there be a
Determined Soul

Let him,
Inspire all young
And direct them to
The new heights of
"What is beauty and
Truth to be"

Time to
Move away from
Violence's and wars;
Emerging as nova
Humans like the
Phoenix

Time to
Defeat old illusions,
Old destructive attitude
And greed-driven milieu
To make room for "Good."

Copyright © 2023 by J.J. Bhatt

Keep
Singing

Where
The world keeps
Shining with your
Love

There is
Always infinite
Joy bringing all the
Meaning to my heart

So sweet heart,
Keep smiling, singing,
Dancing forever for
You're my beauty
And truth

Dear Love,
You're
My possibilities
And meaning of life

Just keep
Smiling, singing, dancing
Forever, forever…forever
In the name of our love…

Copyright © 2023 by J.J. Bhatt

Life is Action

Fear
No more for we're
Going to die anyway

Let us
Instead be a force
Of Good

While rolling
Through the rough
Terrain, it's better to
Leave a legacy:

"We did our
Best to let children
Leave many good
Tomorrows"

Never forget,
"This road to the
Sweet death is
A silent passage to
Eternity...

Copyright © 2023 by J.J. Bhatt

Waiting Dreams

If
Insane human
Transforms into
A universal spirit of
"Oneness"

He shall
Bring a beautiful
Heaven here on
This Planet Blue

There would
Be fresh air to breath,
Clean water to drink and
Quality food to eat

As a
Consequence,
There shall
Emerge humanity of
Melody, meaning and
Rhythm

Children
Shall roam the
World with all joy
And no grief at all…

Copyright © 2023 by J.J. Bhatt

Life-Force

Time to
Wake-up from
Deep slumber

Time to
Be free of
False narratives

Time to
Erase of habits
Of hatred and
Violence

Let us
Wake-up to
Our collective
Common sense

Let us
Be brave and
Reaffirm,

"How to change
Our human nature;
Giving good life to the
Children."

Copyright © 2023 by J.J. Bhatt

Nemesis

"I" is just
Another worm
Walking through my
Time

"I" just
Another spark
From All that is and,
Still looking for
My worth

That is been
The story of every
Searching being and

That is been
The struggle of every
Who's born in human
Form

All
Caught into the
World of turmoil
For forgetting
The very moral
Roots…

Copyright © 2023 by J.J. Bhatt

Being &
Future

Today,
I see them playing,
Running around and
Giggling with alacrity
And so much innocence

They're the
Live hope of their
Parental big dreams, and
They're the treasure of
Their love

Soon
They'll grow-up to be
Teens and fighting for
Identity all right

Even they'll fall in
Love and learn a lesson
Or two

On entering the
Grown-up world, most would
Fall in the line all along the
Traditional path, and

Only a few would
Dare question the path
Where the world is heading
And seeking,
" How to save it in time…"

Copyright © 2023 by J.J. Bhatt

Grand
Unity

Being is
Eternally suspended
Into the transcendent
Experience

He can't be
Separated from it
All for there remains
Only One Truth

"Nothing   is on its
Own in this holistic
Reality called, "All
That is"

Let the
Noble mission of
"Oneness" assail over
The universal theme

Time to know
The reality from higher
Dimensions; connecting
The Social and the
Cosmic Order being
One only."

Copyright © 2023 by J.J. Bhatt

Pulses

While
Walking through
The path of love, laughter
And big ambition

Let every
Human awakens to
His/her meaning

Let it
Be the pulses of
Every human's moral
Intention to act

Yes,
It got to be the very
Mission of every willing
Human to sustain
"Goodness"

Let
Every sentient
Keep walking through
His/her own beauty and
Truth and be worthy of
The journey on hand…

Copyright © 2023 by J.J. Bhatt

Direction

This is the
Time to groom
Young, and

Let them
Be the compelling
Narrative of their
Moral adventure

Let's
Show them the
Direction,

"What is so
Significant to be
Living, today"

Give them
Infinite courage
Teach them,
Social responsibility;
Benefiting the
Whole…

Copyright © 2023 by J.J. Bhatt

Declaration

At the very
Height of alacrity,
We cried,
"Life what a splendid
Myriad possibilities"

Reckoning such
A truth for the
First time,

We just kept
Dancing
Under the canopy
Of the starry night

In such a
Glowing state of our
Awareness, we declared,

"Let there be
Crooked trails
To walk through
Yet, we must remain
Adamant to our set
Noble Goal...

Copyright © 2023 by J.J. Bhatt

Parallel Reality

Being human
Means to be
Suspended
Between order
And disorder

Also means,
Being is the
Manifest
Uncertainty
Indeed

In such a
State of existence,
"Who is he and
Who is he not?"

Against
Such an
Inconvenient
Truth,

Let him
Explore and
Discover,

"His genuine
Identity & the
Noble mission."

Copyright © 2023 by J.J. Bhatt

Odyssey

Sublimity of
Moral being is a necessity
To be free from vanity,
Greed and solipsism

Let it
Be the reckoning, and
Let it be the renewal of
Our humanity, our dignity
And our clarity

Let our
Collective boldness and
Determined will;
Giving us strength to
Overcome all obstacles

Let the
Sublimity of our thought
Be the genuine truth, "Who
Were and what we can become."

Copyright © 2023 by J.J. Bhatt

Destiny Calling

Don't wait,
But lift
This curtain of
The dark destiny,
At once

Don't
Ignore, but act
Soon before you
Walk
Toward the waited
Dreams

Don't pretend
That you know the
Direction
To the "Self-truth"

Be a
Discoverer,
Be your own man, and
Quit apathy that's holding
You back for a very long…

Copyright © 2023 by J.J. Bhatt

Rear View

It's been
Sometime since you
Bid "Goodbye"

It's been
So long; no breeze swept
Across from your heart
To mine

It was
Too hasty to judge the
Outcome of our mutual
Trust and friendship

Oh yes,
Years have gone by
And our world changed
So much

Love leaves
Fingerprints of memory
That never dries, even
The time stole the big
Dream

Love,
Once a high mountain
Of hope, harmony and
Laughter... now crumbled
Into a flat terrain of shattered
Feelings...

Copyright © 2023 by J.J. Bhatt

Being &
Existence

Existence but
A constant moving,
Evolving, spinning
Experience

There is
No escape but to
Keep grinding through
Its merciless rules

Existence,
Always
A brief moment,
Yet forcing to take
A long thought

Existence,
What gauntlet
Thrown at every
Born human

Existence,
What a brief
Moment between
Birth & Death to
Be remembered well…

Copyright © 2023 by J.J. Bhatt

The Gist

Thinkers, saints
And historians cautioned
About human conditions,
Relationships and challenges
In each age

Yet, the old habits
Of the rulers, politicians
And the corporate cultures;
Sadly hasn't changed

Whence
Human suffering and
Despair continues even
In the modern age of
So-called, "Freedom"

That's been
The grand story of the
Irrational humans from
The very beginning

Time to escape
The stubborn curse,
Time to know the core
Cause.... Time to wake-up
And walk together for
The Good of the whole...

Copyright © 2023 by J.J. Bhatt

Synopsis

Let's
Awaken value of
Human courtesy and
Ethical being within

Time to
Sing glory of the
Quest, and inking the
Glorious story at once

Time to
Stand-up tall and
Inspire the young to
Go after their noble
Goal

Yes,
Let them fearlessly
Roll forward
For a greater cause;
"Lifting humanity to the
Apotheosized state…"

Copyright © 2023 by J.J. Bhatt

Deathless

I lived
Long years
And it all came and
Gone like a wisp

Surely,
I am now at the
Renewed dimension,
And am ready to take
Off the edge

I mean, am
Only moment to
Moment while
Contemplating,

"When shall I
Transcend to nova
Dimension,

Where
Another unknown
Called,
"I" must be waiting"

Copyright © 2023 by J.J. Bhatt

Only in Love

Dear love,
We draw strength
From inspiration of
Our deep feelings

Yes, that's the
Source of our dignity
As lovers and

Still we're
Struggling to attain
Our waited dream

Only from
The strong bond of
Trust and confidence,
We shall make it through,
All right

Let's not lose
The track we've been
On for a long

Let's not
Go off the sphere of
The vows we took long
Ago; dear heart...

Copyright © 2023 by J.J. Bhatt

Great
Escape

Let the
Whole world come
Together and declare,

"Time to wake-up
From
The deep slumber, and
Take the torch and March
Forward"

Let the
Moral courage guide us
To keep
Rolling along a right path

Don't be fearful of
Any divinely sanction or
Be afraid of any retribution

Just keep Marching
Forward with open vision
And rational intention

Come let's
Not be governed by the
Man-made beliefs; learn to
Be smart free thinkers and
Define the destiny today…

Copyright © 2023 by J.J. Bhatt

Big
Picture

No point
In turning life into
A tale of humiliation

Don't turn
It into a realm of
"No moral sense, and
Irrational occurrences
Of violence's and wars"

Alternatively,
There is the
Future holding endless
Beauty and truth yet to
Be experienced

Let the
Children feel secured
And happy in their world
Of dreams and best wishes

Time to
Go off the path of senseless
Destructions and deaths, and
Know the real truth,
"Why we're here for…"

Copyright © 2023 by J.J. Bhatt

Soaring Beauty

So what
We all have to
Leave the world when
The call is in

So what
If they ask me to
Drop all my thoughts
And be on the team of
"Global Spirit"

Let it
Be our freedom.
Let it
Be our commitment.
Let it
Be our meaning in it
All

Don't
Complaint
Don't
Impose old views
That never worked

Just fearlessly
Walk toward your destiny
Of "Good" and be the hero
Of your integrity of the mind…

Copyright © 2023 by J.J. Bhatt

Unresolved

Why
Almighty let a few
Greedy rule the world;
Leaving the masses to be
The slaves?

Why
Almighty let young
Die in wars to serve the
Big ambitions of a few
Power hungry of their
Time

Why did
He let human reduced
From great soul to be
Destroyer and killer of
Many million deaths

Why
Today, humans have
Become addicted to the
Techno-lazy and the
Hedonistic life styles
While neglecting their
Ultimate freedom?

Copyright © 2023 by J.J. Bhatt

Beware

Much of the
History is left with
Many million deaths
And destructions

In the name
Of glories after glories,
"Whatever madness was
Claimed each time"

Only a few
Great souls stood to
Stop them, but they
Couldn't

The tide of
Violence's and
Obsession of their
Myopic claims killed
Humanity inch by inch

That is
The past we've been
Carrying today, and
If ignored,

The same old
Saga shall be read
Tomorrow by
Our loving children,
Also!

Copyright © 2023 by J.J. Bhatt

Here & Beyond

On crossing
This turbulent world,
We shall enter into a
New domain

Where
Moral code is a
Reality, and perspicuity
Is a norm than
An exception

In such a
Metaphysical
Essence,

All shall be
Clarified,
And a new human
Spirit shall shine on
The scene

At that point,
All differences shall
Be resolved and
The collective
Dream shall turn into
Reality in an instant…

Copyright © 2023 by J.J. Bhatt

Love

When
We're unknown
To one another,

Only
Dreams were the
Silent link between
Our throbbing hearts

When
We accidently collided
In a big party,
You seemed
First annoyed and soon
You forgave me

Well, that
Was the beginning of
Our journey together

As we danced
Cheek to cheek under
The canopy of the starry
Nights

We're illuminated
To love more and more,
Yes more and more as
Our journey lasted with
Every new beginning
Since then…

Copyright © 2023 by J.J. Bhatt

Final Step

When
Meditating in the
Tranquility of all that is,
I hear only the sound of
The universal soul

No He ain't the
Supernatural being, but
The totality of all that
Is never been claimed

That is the
Theater of ultimate
Wisdom

That is the
End of all journeys
Of an intelligent being

That is the
Source of the silent
Moral beginning

That is the
Realm we must
Experience on our own,

And
Not in the name of
Any falsely claimed
Conceptualized Thought…

Copyright © 2023 by J.J. Bhatt

Ultimate
Glow

I am
Gone from the
Reality what we know,
"What is being here?"

I am no
More a label of
"My self-identity"

I am just
A Soul, albeit a
Cosmic spark

Came to
Understand the
Meaning of the
Spinning Great Wheel

Now,
My times up and
That is the
Ultimate freedom

That is the
Ultimate meaning,
"Who am I, and
Why "I" is the
Eternal consciousness…"

Copyright © 2023 by J.J. Bhatt

Higher Dimension

When
I close my eyes
And stay steady
Thoughtless

There
Emerges an
Awesome beauty of
The entire universe

At that very
Turning point,
"I am no more"

There is
No darkness.
There is no
Turbulence, there
Is only effloresce
Bliss

That is
Where I know,
"I am my soul," and

That is when
I experience, my
"Holistic connection
To all that is indeed…"

Copyright © 2023 by J.J. Bhatt

Life 101

Well,
That's the way
Life rolls always

It's merciless,
Its struggles and
Corrections, and
It's all ignorance

Yet,
Life is the only
Mother that got
The power to give
Love, laughter
And hope too

Life
Demands,
"Either shape-up
Or shape outré"
For there is
No in-between

Life gives
Freedom, and
Same life can
Steal it too!

Copyright © 2023 by J.J. Bhatt

The
Move

Looking
The past
In retrospective,
There is not much
To be inspired

So here
We're, the historic
Experience; still
Ascending toward
A point unknown

And
Keep wondering,
"If the direction is
Either right or wrong"

While the
Future is barreling
Over our
Collective unsure heads

Time to
Get smart. Time to
Believe in ourselves and
Time to team-up and make
A big difference in the
Name of good…

Copyright © 2023 by J.J. Bhatt

Validation

We've
Witnessed great
Strength of woman in
Our mothers, sisters, wives,
Daughters time after time

Many
Are moving forward
As leaders in armed forces,
Corporate world and serving
In many different good ways

Oh yes,
Woman, mother
Who sustains humanity
Through love, care and
Many sacrifices

Women,
Yet to gain their
Full potentials
Women,
Yet to express,
Full freedom

Women be
Fully validated by the
Modern Neanderthals
Who still control their,
"Dos and don'ts…"

Copyright © 2023 by J.J. Bhatt

Zenith

We're the
Finite awareness à la
Soaring beauty heading
Toward the world of
Perfection

As we
Fly; leaving
Behind all emotions
Passions and capricious
Opinions

I mean,
Dropping subjective
Interpretations, and the
Constant struggles to
Quest for truth

Let it
Be a genuine journey
Toward the world of
Our meaning

Let it
Be the highest goal
To be experienced

While
Ascending to the
Total tranquility, rhythm
And full understanding
Of the Self.

Copyright © 2023 by J.J. Bhatt

50th

As cool
Zephyr swept
Through
The lofty Mount

Bringing in
Many lost memories
Back to my young
Heart

It's the same
Mount where we
Took the first hike

Yes,
To conquer
That impossible
Challenge and make
It through it all

Well, to us
Young blood then, it
Was a child's play and

Voila we did
Kiss the highest
Peak and declared,

"We were the
Determined lovers all
The way to meet our
Waited dream today!"

Copyright © 2023 by J.J. Bhatt

Mercy

Where is
The destination
While being lost
Walking along
The zigzag trail

What's
The direction
While trying to be
Free from the world
Of conflict,
Bickering and crazy
Whims

Why do we
Still keep fighting,
Hating, killing many
Of our genetic cousins

Why are we
Keep destroying
Dearest Mother;
Nourishing our breath,
Thirst… hunger every
Night and day!

Copyright © 2023 by J.J. Bhatt

The
Song

Life may be
Nothing but the
Emotional intensity
Of every born

Life,
What an incredible
Fulfillment to hold
Onto love and dream

Life,
Only venue where
Grief and joy keeps
Singing now and then

Life,
Where
Every human's
Moral will is measured;
Minute by minute while
Ride is on…

Copyright © 2023 by J.J. Bhatt

Assessment

It's
Understanding that
Defines first step
Of the journey ahead

It's
Measure of the moral
Courage that balances
One's character

Don't let
Time slip away too
Soon, and don't let the
Focus be lost while on
The rough trail

Let's learn
To observe, "Silence"
Like the monks;

Permitting
"What is individual's
Social responsibility to
Realize a world of peace,
Harmony and hope…."

Copyright © 2023 by J.J. Bhatt

Inspiration

No regret,
No grief and no
Guilt to report

Only "I" is
Freewill born
To keep the trail
Open all the
Way to the end

Why
Waste life in tears,
Despairs and million
Sorry when the light is
So ubiquitous

Why
Keep bowing down
To all preaching's,
Restraints and stubborn,
But dividing isms

Let us be
Free humans who
Must keep enjoying
Our respective splendid
Self-essence…

Copyright © 2023 by J.J. Bhatt

Affirmation

Go steady
While the killer
Storm is hovering over
Your journey at this
Time

Stay steady
With the purpose
Even when "Nay
Sayers" insist you
Can't

Against
All odds, never lose
Grace and calm
For the trail is full of
Many turning points

Just sustain and
Strengthen with
Positivity and courage

Let every
Success welcomes
I with a big smile…

Copyright © 2023 by J.J. Bhatt

Timeless

In this
12'by 12'petite office
Where I spend most of
My mornings to express
A few revolving thoughts

I am not alone,
But surrounded by the
Pictorial memories of folks
With whom I had walked
Million miles

Indeed,
It is my very sacred
Humble place, where I had
Meditated many hours;
Seeking
"What is it all about?"

Oh this
Tiny room full of
Endless memories always
Making me feel,

"As if I am still
Walking along with them for
They've never left my rolling
Memories ever…"

Copyright © 2023 by J.J. Bhatt

Rolling Drum

Life,
What a fascinating
Adventure indeed

Where
"Trials and Errors"
Keep revolving every
Minute

Where
We're "Lost and
Found," time after
Time

Life,
What an eternal
Curiosity, creativity;
Holding onto our
Ephemeral worldview

Oh yes,
Life always a
Frictional rolling
Drum of history,

We yet
To know, "How to
Escape from its
Blunders and sins."

Copyright © 2023 by J.J. Bhatt

Identity
& Mission

Life
May be forever
In memories or the
Digital prints

That got to
Be the scope and
Limit of us mortal
Being

Nothing
Shall be owned
Forever; save for
The "Good Deeds"
Left behind

If that be
The Truth,
"We're the aliens
In transition from
Temporal to eternal,
In the spiritual sense,
I suppose!"

Copyright © 2023 by J.J. Bhatt

Measure

Measure of
Measure of human
Courage and integrity

Indeed,
Is the measure,
When human alone
Is the owner of his/her
Volition and destiny,
At all time

Don't
Let others governed
Your thoughts or
Disrupt the core essence

Be proud of
Your heritage, cultural
ID and be confident

While
Walking through the
Trail and leaving it open
To the young to be inspired
Like you…

Copyright © 2023 by J.J. Bhatt

Transformation

In a
Strict sense,
Sentient must be the
Time travelers

Whose heading
From chaos to the
Silent order, and

From
Blind belief to
The meaningful
Endeavor simply

In other words,
Sentient are stationed
For a while to learn,

"What be
Their conducts to
Build a better world
For the new born"

Let it be
Understood,
"Sheer ignorance never
Grants a *Carte blanche*
To enter the so-called,
"Heavenly experience!"

Copyright © 2023 by J.J. Bhatt

Flexed Feelings

It's been
Love all the way
Since we began the
Great voyage

Yes,
It's been
Long since we
Began singing the
"Love forever"

Let's
Enjoy this magic
Experience

Let's
Do something
"Larger than whom
We're?"

Let's
Share the selfless
Love with all others
Of our time

Come let's
Awaken the whole
World, "Love is the pulse
Of every human and
Shall be many tomorrows too…"

Copyright © 2023 by J.J. Bhatt

Live,
Well

When
Each is reborn
With integrity, simplicity
And clarity

There shall
Emerge a divinely force
Of humanity itself on the
Blessed scene

So,
Let's awaken our
Common sense and lit
The sincerity of
Coexistence

Let's drop
Diseases of
Bigotry, violence's and
Fragmented pseudo claims

Time to
Grow up. Time to feel
The beauty of humanity,
First hand

Time to
Rewrite the future of
Billion plus kids, and learn
To be in an eternal peace…

Copyright © 2023 by J.J. Bhatt

Moral Necessity

Never be
Afraid of having a
Rendezvous with
Mr. Noble Death

It's just an
Opening to another
Realm where new
Pages of history yet
To be written

Never
Fear another human
Either he/she's high or
Mighty, or simply totally
Drowned in hypocrisy

For you're
Indeed the master of
Your journey, albeit a
Definer of your destiny

Let every
Young brave gather-up
Inner strength, and

Keep
Fearlessly going upward
While holding the set
Mission of the self-truth…

Copyright © 2023 by J.J. Bhatt

Prologue

Love is
Fire that keeps the
Journey of two lovers
Through the light and
The dark

Love is
Beautiful feelings that
Got to be seized by every
Human indeed

"Love, love…love"
All that is needed by the
Hungry humanity at each
Step of its way to freedom

If the
Whole is dipped into
The nectar of love,
Peace would be just
A norm and not
An exception

No need to
Wait for any divinely
Blessings, but to enjoy
Heavenly spirit right here
On this wonderful Planet
Blue indeed…

Copyright © 2023 by J.J. Bhatt

Be Inspired

Let the
Young build a world
Where civility, national
Identity and pride of heritage,
Keeps humming every
Whichever way

Let it
Be a growing universal
Spirit among young to
Strengthen faith and fidelity
To the well-being of the
Whole

Only then
Humans shall arrive at
The right place and in time;
Experiencing their collective,
"Wisdom"

Outside of it,
Mostly life is propelled by
Falsity, tribalism, hypocricy
And an ever insatiable greed…

Time to
Stitch the worn out fabric
Before it's too late…

Copyright © 2023 by J.J. Bhatt

The Guide

Only
True lovers enjoy
Significance of
Their essence

Only the
True time travelers
Know the meaning of
Their journey all right

Only the
Awakened souls
Shall comprehend the
Validity of their being in
Human form

Yes,
Only the young
Minds shall have
Time to decipher,

"All the
Hidden blunders and sins
Of the past; setting up a
Futuristic new blueprint
Called, "Good."

Copyright © 2023 by J.J. Bhatt

Silent Soul

We mustn't be
Concern neither
The magical divine nor
The mystical Unknown

For our
Battle isn't with them,
But the "Self" itself

Let the
Creative mind keeps
Evolving through,
"Self-Realization"

Let him
Grasp intricacies of
"What is and what is not?"
While rolling along the
Assigned time

Not to be
Concern neither with
Cacophony nor
Trivialities of the
Quotidian existence

Let the
"Silent Soul" guide the
Monkey mind through the
Dark terraine all right…

Copyright © 2023 by J.J. Bhatt

81

Being Human

"I," an
Eternal expression
Who is actually
A mystical spark
From the cosmic
Fire that's been on

"I,"
Essentially born
To drop ignorance, and
Be free

From
Unnecessary
Imposed superstitions,
Myths and
Myopic beliefs

That's why
It's relevant to grasp
"Who am I and what I
Ought to be"

"I" what an
External projection of
My soul, strengthened
By the moral being,
Within... life after life...

Copyright © 2023 by J.J. Bhatt

Truth
As Is

At birth
We're all equal
In innocence

Indeed,
There is only
"Pure Good" and
Loving maternal
Care

We're
Also equal at death
When all seems to be
One big dream

It's the
Journey in-between
Is the real measure
Of our worth

Where
Nothing is certainty,
But the little luck and
Mostly the self-endeavor
Is the determinant

That's where
Individual freedom
Gets in action, and it's
Called, "Making choices…"

Copyright © 2023 by J.J. Bhatt

All in Flux

Forever is
Either here or may
Be never

Yet
All that keeps
Revolving in the
Mind only

The Sun is
Shining today, but
May not tomorrow

Humans are
Here for a brief, but
Eternal may be
Somewhere else

That be
The spinning
Uncertainty; soaring
Through the flux

Oh that
Curiosity of the
Evolving human being!

Oh that
Creative imagination
Exploring, "The meaning
Of him in perpetuity…"

Copyright © 2023 by J.J. Bhatt

The
Glow

That
Rising flow…
That rising high
Tide; lifting spirit
Of all dreams

Indeed,
That ever glows,
Yes that cosmic
Spark is the new
Born human

Who's
Destined to be
Endless possibilities,
An all the star lights
To shine forever

Let the
Child begin
Ascending as an
Evolving truth
From here to
Eternity and

Let him leave a
Legacy of good
Behind; fulfilling the
Noble Mission in
The end…

Copyright © 2023 by J.J. Bhatt

New Reality

When I
Graze infinity
That's been
Powered by countless
Stars, galaxies and
Riddles

I am
Not deterred by
Such magnificent
Amazement

For am here
To decipher the
Enigmatic existence

And
Be liberated
From the dark clouds
Of violence's, bigotry,
Wars and much more

Indeed, am born
Here to affirm,,
"What a
Noble is the journey
What an incredible
Is the destiny"

Copyright © 2023 by J.J. Bhatt

Let it
Happen

Its okay
To be drawn
Toward emerging
Romance between
Two searching hearts,
Always

Of course,
It's okay to swim
With courage through
The turbulent love
Affairs, always

Don't
Fight the feelings,
If the throbs are on
An equal wavelength

Don't
Kill the moment, if
Trust and joy are quite
Intact

It's always
Okay to fall in love
When destiny calls for
It with a pure luck or
Not!

Copyright © 2023 by J.J. Bhatt

Noblesse Oblige!

Under the
Lenses of high
Resolution of an
Haute monde societal
Circle

There is
A veneer of niceness,
But the abyss of vanity
And hypocricy remains

Under
Their glittered jewelries
And opulent palatial
Life style, there is a
Hidden insecurity as well

Yet,
They're the champs
Who thrive by their
Big names, wealth and
Power to call the shots

Surprisingly,
Preachers, politicians,
Academicians and the
Rest succumbs to their
Indirect demands, killing
The true freedom…

Copyright © 2023 by J.J. Bhatt

Greetings!

There is
A silent
Movement from
Confusion to clarity

Let there
Be a way
to free from
Contradictions and
Paradoxes

And,
Let there be a
Path to be calm
And alert through
Disciplined mind

Let humanity,
Simply ascend to
It's set social order;
Tailored for harmony
And peace...

Copyright © 2023 by J.J. Bhatt

Be
Fearless

Don't doubt,
Don't hesitate, but
Dare to ask question

Don't care
What others may say,
Or criticize; fearlessly
Fulfill your curiosity
To the end

Don't swallow
Man-made beliefs of
Lies, violence and
Senseless bloodshed

Be smart and
Know the very essence,
"Who you're and what's
The way to march on…"

Copyright © 2023 by J.J. Bhatt

Love
By Chance

It's a
Beautiful cool
Evening

As the
Sun ready
To sink beneath
The horizon

There is
Calm and only
The swells quietly
Hitting the shore

Soon,
The Moonlit shall
Shine saying, "Sweet
Hello"

Yes, dear heart,
It's time to sing and
Dance by the mighty
Blue Sea, once again

And this is
Where we'd kissed
For the first time…

Copyright © 2023 by J.J. Bhatt

History Singing

We're
But the collective
Historic projection;

Passing
Through the light
And the dark of our
Thoughts, words and
deeds

Whenever we
Created, "Good,"
There was glory and
The Sun shone
Everywhere

Whenever we
Imposed false
Narrative in His name
Triggering wars and
Genocides; burying us
Under the holy hell

As the
Old lady, "History"
Continues to sing
"Either we wake-p and be
Illuminated or stay in the
Suffering mode?"

Copyright © 2023 by J.J. Bhatt

Arise

What's the
Point being called,
"Intelligent Being?"

If we
Never escape from the
Slavery of the subjective
Interpretative Great
Sphere

What's the
Rationale being,
"H. *sapiens,* a la human
The wise," When we can't
Meet such a lofty goal?"

What's the
Reason to be born
When we don't dare to
Reform our old habits of
The stubborn mind

Time to
Think smart. Time to
Wake-up and roll toward
Adventure of "Good"…

Copyright © 2023 by J.J. Bhatt

Being &
Immortality

This
Accidental being,
Always a continuum
Of the ancestral stock

Thus an immortal
Genetic flow from one
Generation to another
May be!

If so,
Why be concerned
About entering either
The hell or the heaven

It's just
A ceaseless flow of
Life after life also called,
"Rebirth or whatever else!"

No need
To fear of any mighty
Force and no need to
Keep on swallowing the
Old dated ways for

It's all about
Comings and Goings,
Irrespective of whatever
"It is or it is not…"

Copyright © 2023 by J.J. Bhatt

Epiphany

Let's
Just imagine,
"We've arrived before
The magnificent holistic
Reality powered by its
Infinite beauty indeed"

And, let's
Just be inspired,
Spontaneously grasping
The true meaning of our
Individual, "Self-Truth"
Simply

Again,
That Self-truth is
The epiphany, "Who
We're and what we ought
To be"

After such a
Mystical flash of a
Noble reckoning, is it
Possible

To lift the
Whole; liberating it
From the curse of the
Seven sin?

Copyright © 2023 by J.J. Bhatt

Profile

Hurray,
It's time to be
Triumphant in
The set game

Hurray,
To be
Triumphant over
The zigzag path

Yes, we
Got to beat all the
Odds and continue
To move fearlessly
Forward at every
Turning point

Whatever
May be the future
Or the discovery
There of?

Come let's
Celebrate the beauty
Of our collective
Awakening at every
Forward step…

Copyright © 2023 by J.J. Bhatt

Contextual

When
I know, "I am a
Contextual being in
The totality of all that is"

It means,
I am standing before
The Eternal inspiration,
What is the source of
My very essence

Come
Share the tranquility
Of deep contemplation
Yes,
Time to awake, arise
And begin to explore,
"What is it all about?"

In this
Otherwise,
World of ignorance,
Arrogance and
Indifferent attitude

Let's relearn,
"How to live life
With a right pursuit
And understanding the
"Self-truth"

Copyright © 2023 by J.J. Bhatt

The Way

Its life
Waiting to be filled
With love, laughter and
A greater purpose,
"To live, but live well"

It's the very
Moment to be seized
With alacrity and
Immeasurable hope

No time
To drop tears and
No time to be in despair

Just keep walking
Along the trail leading
To harmony and joy

Yes, the
Trail to be left open
For the young to explore,
To understand and to seek
Their genuine inner being,
At last…

Copyright © 2023 by J.J. Bhatt

Betrayal

Again, I said,
"Don't leave these
Beautiful feelings
We've been sharing
For a long"

Again and
Again, I return to
Know, "Why did you
Run away so soon?"

Thought,
We'd conquer the
World

Thought,
We're rewriting
The story of
Our eternal love

Oh, you fool,
"Why did you get off
The track so soon?"

Let
The echoes of
My song touches
Your guilty heart
Again and over again…

Copyright © 2023 by J.J. Bhatt

Looking Forward

Let the quest of
Beauty and truth
Be the very experience
While we're passing
Through this complex
Reality all right

Let's be
Coherent with our
Thoughts, words, and
Choices while we journey
Through it all

Let's
Not leave any lose
End to let evil doers spoil
The moral adventure we've
Been on

Knowing so well,
Our kind is in turmoil and
Trying to overcome
Many insane "Isms"

It's time,
We come together and
Begin to seek solution
To our existential issue
From this point on…

Copyright © 2023 by J.J. Bhatt

Perspective

Human means
A fearless will who
Ceaselessly evolves
From imperfection
To Perfection

That's why,
He is resolute to
Ascend from ignorance
To the self-awareness
While being here

If so, his
Existence is powered
By the right purpose at
Every step of the way

Let the
Moral will jolts him
Out of the deep slumber,

And let him
Reach out to the highest
Goal of his illumined mind,
At last…

Copyright © 2023 by J.J. Bhatt

Forever

Never
We shall be separated
From the vows of our
Deep love

Neither
Any challenge nor
Even death shall ever
Dare to split our
Single heart

For we've
Endured many births
And rebirths and the
Bond is impossible to
Break

We're two
Sacred souls who've
Become, "One," and

No way
To separate us for
Our journey's been
In eternity ever since
We fell in love...

Yes,
Dear heart, we're
The lovers in love
Forever,
Forever...forever...

Copyright © 2023 by J.J. Bhatt

World
As Is

All that
Glittered and the
Set palatial lifestyle
Where
They meet and
Greet every week

And silently
Reinforcing their social
Rankings and settling
Few secret deals

That's the
Modus operandii of
Rich and famous seeking
Big profits, power
And control over the
System

No wonder,
There is de facto
World of "Have ones
Few and have not's by
The many billions?"

Copyright © 2023 by J.J. Bhatt

Killer Storm

It's been
Raining for
Days

The Seas
Gone mad as the
Storm surges hit
The shore

So hard;
Destroying
Million dreams,
In an instant

It's been
Sunless realm for
Many days and there's
No communications as
Electricity no more

What a
Great tragedy,
The killer storm never
Leaves the diabolic
Habit of the mind…

Copyright © 2023 by J.J. Bhatt

Surprise, Surprise!

That's
The way life
Rolls sometime slow
And sometime
Not so

That's
The way love
Evolves sometime
Good and sometime
Not so

We're
Born walkers and
We keep walking
From one opinion to
Many and back to the
Same again in time

We're
The lost tribe who's
Been looking for a
Deep meaning and

Still unable
To succeed to meet
The mission called,
"The common sense
Awareness…"

Copyright © 2023 by J.J. Bhatt

Grand
Flow

What
I think is the
Expression of my
Life to roll

What
I believe is the
Inner strength that
Shows the way

That's the
Reality of my being
Alive while
I pursue my worth

That's the
Gusto of my precious
Self while I chug
Along through the
Set challenges of
My time

What I've
Understood must
Define my path, and
My freedom at every
Turning point…

Copyright © 2023 by J.J. Bhatt

Mystical Love

It's
A world of
Endless feelings;
Upwelling from the
Prodigious depth,
And it's called,
"Pure Love"

It's
A deep source
Of trust and
Commitment
Between two hearts
Destined to be one
Forever

Indeed,
It's the mirror of
Our joint destiny
It's the story of
Our eternal love for
Ours to come

Love,
What an irresistible
Life force; evolving
Toward a perfection of
Two mystical souls…

Copyright © 2023 by J.J. Bhatt

Reset

Man
Mustn't be alienated
From life even if
It doesn't have all the
Right answers

I mean,
He mustn't be thrown
Into unconscious despair,
Even if there is total
Absence of sincerity

Let's
Bring in a milieu of
Goodwill and
Understanding who're
Lost in the unfair world

Let's give them
Hope and courage, and

Let them know,
"Many billions are also
Struggling one way or other
Just like them while
On the road to worthiness…"

Copyright © 2023 by J.J. Bhatt

Time &
Place

We're
The extended finite
Flares from the magnifique
Reality in essence

We're
In a long quest to grasp,
"What is the meaning to
Be in this imperfect state
Of the mind?"

Is it
The forgotten connectivity
With the totality, "All That
Is or what?'

Is it
The failure to know
The human Contextuality
Or what?

Is it
Apathy to launch a
Creative dialogue to unveil,
"Our collective truth or not!"

Copyright © 2023 by J.J. Bhatt

Noble
Path

We're
Born to redefine
Our significance in
This grand chaotic
Existence

Yes,
Each is a
Potential spiritual
Inspiration;
Journeying between
Life and death

Time
To take
Responsibility
To honor civility,
And to restrained
Arrogant conduct…

Copyright © 2023 by J.J. Bhatt

New
Zeal

Cheer up
Friends,

Time to
Reckon value of
Our being here

Time
To drop the old
Myopia and phobia
And fearlessly
Move on

Yes,
Time to be
Reborn with a
New zeal and
Determined will

Come lets
Bring in
Necessary
Social order and
Good meaning,
"Who we're?"

Copyright © 2023 by J.J. Bhatt

Triumphant

Along a
Smooth icy surface;
Skating, what a great
Thrill

Climbing
A high mount with
A right skill gives
So much
Confidence

And sailing
Through a calm sea
Is a great experience,
Indeed

While
Living through life
With positivity and
Empathy is the
Best human to be

Seems,
While journeying
Through
Uncertainty must be
The genuine trial
Existence…

Copyright © 2023 by J.J. Bhatt

That's
Life

It was a
Small town then
Where I grew-up and
Began exploring it's
Bucolic beauty and the
Good folks

Though young,
Intuitively I understood,
"How all was near perfection
As people cared for one
Another so well"

Yes,
That's the memory
Keeps recurring time
After time while I move
Through the life in the
21st

Sometimes,
The past is
Inspiring and
Sometimes it's not,

Well,
That's life, *c'est la vie*
Forever and I must
Keep moving on…

Copyright © 2023 by J.J. Bhatt

Nova
Future

Away, away,
Please be away from
The bad memories of
Bloody wars

No point
In listening over and
Again those sinful acts
Of man

No point
In reading inglorious
Pages of history, if they
Keep repeating time and
Time again

Let our
Collective
Moral necessity
Rid off the hellish
State of war-mongering
Mindset, and

Be the
Real heroes of
The Noble Peace for
A change...

Copyright © 2023 by J.J. Bhatt

Legacy

Peace it-self
Is the morality in
Action and

Every human
Looking for it is
On the right track

Let the
Guardians, preachers
And educators get
Busy

To open-up
Such a milieu; defining
A meaningful life to live
For the young of today

Indeed,
For many generations
To habitat the Blue Planet
With a gratitude to their
"Elders"

If we
Succeed today, we shall
Fulfill our collective
Moral responsibility of many
Tomorrows; shining forever...

Copyright © 2023 by J.J. Bhatt

A Point

Our struggles are
But a reconciliation,
Between "Who we're and
What we ought to become"

That's the
Reality we've been
Passing through since
The beginning

It's been also
Great challenge
Between
"Our freedom and
Social responsibility"

Each is born
To reciprocate morality
With others and nature
Itself; meeting criteria
Of being enlightened

Let there be
Understanding,
Love, tolerance and

Let there be
Awareness,
"We're here to
Cleanse the corrupt
Mind, essentially..."

Copyright © 2023 by J.J. Bhatt

Our
Time

Time to
Challenge
"Globalization;"
Sucking up enormous
Natural resources to satiate
Ever demanding consumers

Excessive
Hedonistic life style
Powered by the
"Globalization" silently
Destroys the spirituality,
Indeed

Consequentially,
Greed, vanity and the
Thick layers of ignorance
Emerge on the daily scene

Not to mention,
Severe damage to Mother
Earth; leading to the
Climate boiling, melting
Many million glaciers and
Human dreams…

Copyright © 2023 by J.J. Bhatt

Illiterates

Humanity
Is an eternal poetry
As it began with the
First thought,
"What is it all about?"

When cave
Dwellers grazed the
Magnifique cosmos;
Spontaneously recited
Their first poem

Letting
Them sing and dance in
Full trance and gusto;
Creating thoughts about
Divinely wonders

Ancient folks
Wrote epic poetry and
Kept the spirituality of
Humanity high and mighty

Today,
In this techno-addicted
Existence, sadly poetry is
No longer the positive force
Inspiring many millions young,
It was once?

Copyright © 2023 by J.J. Bhatt

Breaking
Point

Myopia
Seems to be the
Sovereign today

Everywhere,
Preachers, teachers
And guardians caught
In that incurable fever

All that projects
Nothing, but the large
Scale anxiety and fear

There is
Chaos as folks aren't
Ready to listen to others;
Only cacophony is the
Prevailing command

There is
Disappearance of
The middle class;
Leaving nothing but a big
Gap between super-wealthy
And million lost on the street…

Copyright © 2023 by J.J. Bhatt

Think Global

All I know,
"We're manifest
Hope, harmony and
Love"

When we
Forget, "Who we're
And what we ought
To be, at that point
We've lost the battle"

Yes,
When we succumb
To the hedonism and
Techno-drug addiction
And ignore the moral
Goodwill, we've lost
The north compass

When
Zealots shore-up
Their tribalism and
Keep imposing false
Narratives on others,

Silently
We lose the
Moral strength and end
Up dying without a
Fulfillment of our dream…

Copyright © 2023 by J.J. Bhatt

Another Realm

If we
Fly over to the
World of imagination,
Reality would be
Different than what
We experience in our
Ordinary existence

In such a
Free realm, nothing
Is an objective thing,
But the ever-changing
Creative whims

It's the
Wonderful world of
Serendipity where new
Perspectives keep
Rolling the curious
Mind

Indeed,
It's the
Deep meditative
Experience, albeit
A spiritual trance;
Triumphing the soul
Over a conceptualized
Divine...

Copyright © 2023 by J.J. Bhatt

Integrity

When
Chaos overwhelms
And all destructive
Forces are at zenith,

Real heroes
Emerge on the ugly
Scene, and inspire
Million young
"

That's been the
Great saga of our kind
As Heroes from all walks
Of life shined on
The historic scene

Let us
Remember
Them through
Endeavors, commitments
An actions, and not just with
Panegyric speeches and
Momentary celebrations...

Copyright © 2023 by J.J. Bhatt

History,
As Is

History
Vividly shown,
"When rulers
Are corrupt, the society
Turns corrupt, and there is
That inevitable downfall
In the end"

No wonder,
Many civilizations
Rose and fell time after
Time, and sadly
The story remains
Pretty much the same
,In a way, "Today?"

"Human
Civilization,"
What a typological
Experience so deeply
Ingrained in the Psyche,
Life after life…

Copyright © 2023 by J.J. Bhatt

Moral Judgment

What's the
Rationale being born
Human,

If we keep
Rotting into despair,
Futility and hopelessness

If such a
State of absurdity continues;
Violence's, wars and bigotry
Would turn into societal norms

Stop the
Insanity now, and let's return
To the higher dimensions of
Our collective humanity,
Our dignity, our civility…our
Morality; soon

Let's not
Succumb to the evil forces
And run away from the noble
Mission we're born for…

Copyright © 2023 by J.J. Bhatt

Bold
Step

Every
Being is the
Constant
Flow of hope,
Courage and
Integrity

Indeed,
Each is a historic
Force of change;

Leaving
A great legacy,
"Good o be"

That's it,
That's the
Journey of the
Human Spirit

Yet to be
Rejuvenated with
Determined will, and
Universal awareness
Of compassion forever…

Copyright © 2023 by J.J. Bhatt

Priority

Don't
Say sorry every time
For it erodes your dignity

Don't
Run away from the
Moral responsibility when
The crisis emerges on the
Scene

Don't keep
Giving excuses now and
Then for it lowers your
Very humanity

Stand-up tall
And gather all you're inner
Strengths, and begin the
Mission with commitment
And courage

For Heaven sake,
Do something worthwhile
To inspire your kids
Who in turn,
Shall gain confidence
To be larger than life..

Copyright © 2023 by J.J. Bhatt

Lit Up!

Time to
Lit up authentic
Being within

Time to
Get on the track
Full of hope, joy
And melody to sing

Cone,
Let's celebrate
Our "Global Spirit"
To move on for
Good

Let's get
Away from the dark
Side of lies, anomalies
And uncertainties

Let's come
Together and save
The Planet Blue and
Billion lives too.

Copyright © 2023 by J.J. Bhatt

Thank You

Dear heart,
Do you remember
When we danced for
The first time

It was
Such a perfect dream;
That turned into reality of
"You and I forever"

Do you
Still remember,
It was a New Year
Celebration and

We
Laughed and dined
And we sang all happy
Songs while dancing
Cheek to cheek

Oh yes babe,
Time never touched us
For we've been dancing
In eternity from the very
Beginning…

Copyright © 2023 by J.J. Bhatt

Portrayal

Life
Amid anguish also
Offers hope, humanity
Dignity and compassion

Life may be
Burden by myriad
Doubts, ambiguities
And vicissitudes, yet,
Reciprocates in
Knowing it's deeper
Meaning

Life
Always a complex
Tale of good and
Evil, right and wrong,
Light and dark
Yet leading us to the
Soaring "Perfection..."

Life
Yet to be fully
Understood and
Validated in terms of
Our gratitude and moral
Courage as ever…

Copyright © 2023 by J.J. Bhatt

Evanescent

From
These ephemeral
Opinions,
Nothing good will
Emerge to resolve the
Great riddles of our
Time

What
A shame, all that is
"Good" seems fading
From the spirit of
Modern man

Even many
Lovers are unable to
Keep their sacred
Vows

As they
Fail to hold on to
The higher purpose
Of their set destiny;
Defeating the very
Meaning of love…

Copyright © 2023 by J.J. Bhatt

Giant
Leap

What if
We lose our
Self identity

And what if,
We manifest,
Mystical essence
On the scene

Will there
Still time left
To innovate, to
Imagine or what?

What if,
We can't survive
In such a realm of
"All that is Perfection!"

Let's not
Then complain being
The struggling forces;

Living
Through so-called,
"Imperfect, unfair and
Rowdy place…

Copyright © 2023 by J.J. Bhatt

Fortitude

As the
Dark clouds barrels
Through all fragile
Dreams and hope

Only my
Soul demands,
I take a bold stand and
Keep the castle safe

Indeed, the
Oncoming storm
Is asking to
Fight its challenge
As well

At that
Inflection, my inner
Being keeps inspiring,
"To take charge and not to
Run away from the killer
Storm"

That's
The way and the only
Royal way to conquer
The fear itself

While I keep
Struggling through my
Own "Trials and
Trepidations, time after
Time …"

Copyright © 2023 by J.J. Bhatt

Love means Courage

So I sing,
"Dear Heart, this is
Our time. This is our
Destiny…this is the
Story of you and I"

I hear,
Clarion bells of
Hope and good
Feelings; ringing
Through and through
Our two throbbing
Hearts tonight

So I ask,
"How long will you
Keep ignoring this
Fast slipping away
Time?"

I say,
"Take a deep
Breath, collect all
Your courage and take
A first fearless step, and
Land into my open arms
And be my forever…."

Copyright © 2023 by J.J. Bhatt

Think, Future

Sooner
We comprehend,
"We're but a continuum
Disharmony and victim of
Gluttonous greed"

Time toll
Locate the real cause,
"Why we've been suffering
So long"

I mean,
Do we understand,
Why million young is
Feeling alienated,
Today?

Albeit, our
Humanity seems
Losing its grip

Through
Rising confusion,
And disorder in this
Ultra modern time

Time,
To seek solutions
Knowing, "Who we're
And what we ought to be…"

Copyright © 2023 by J.J. Bhatt

Impossible, Possible!

Ultimate
Quest of truth got to
Be in conquering the
Human mind only

Let it be
The final goal
Of every human who's
Seeking to live in the
World of "Good"

Let each
Drop his/her greed,
Vanity and revenge

Let each
Drop his/her falsity,
Irrational belief and
Learn to extend hand
To others

Let us
Collectively fight for
Freedom from violence's,
Wars and techno-mind-
Controlling- machines…

Copyright © 2023 by J.J. Bhatt

Liberation

Let's roll
Toward a direction
Where wonders of life
Unfold regularly

Yes,
Where joyous
Soul keeps transforming
Wishes and dreams into
Reality of happiness

Let's
Reset the moral
Frequencies, and be
In harmony leading to the
Ultimate illumination
Soon

May the
Entire humanity
Reverberates, the wild
World with the inspiring
Hymn,

"OM Shanti,
OM Shanti" and be
Liberated from trivialities
And falsity at once...

Copyright © 2023 by J.J. Bhatt

Watch
Out!

We think,
"We're individual"
But for survival, we
Need to be together

Yes, to be
The triumphant
Heroes of Good over
Evil always

Let's
Remember,
"We're a
Weak animals"

Time
To join hands and
Think of our collective
Survival being a unique
Oneness

Look,
Our Planet is dying,
Climate is threatening,
Nukes are piling up and
AIs etc are threatening
Our future

We're running
Out of time and we're
Forgetting, "Who we're
And what's the mission
Yet to be?"

Copyright © 2023 by J.J. Bhatt

Juggernaut

Life,
What an inspiring
Reality where beauty
And good must rule
The monkey mind

Life is the
Time to transcend
From darkness to
Illumination

Life is the
Chance to roll from
Tragedy to comedy,
May be

Life,
What a glorious
Book of every born,
Who lived and gone

Life,
Always a base
Reference from where
Every being is measured,
Time after time…

Copyright © 2023 by J.J. Bhatt

My Magic

Dear Heart,
It's only in love,
Our feelings, dreams
And reality becomes
One

Love,
What a mystical
Magic of two waiting
Souls willing to be
One

Dear Heart,
"You've brought
Forth trust, dignity
And integrity at once"

Yes,
Your love has
Defined our "Spiritual
Quest toward Perfection,
Indeed."

Copyright © 2023 by J.J. Bhatt

Eternity

It's through
The flow of consciousness,
Human is both spatio-temporal
And eternal at the same
Time

That is the
Anthrocosmic connectivity
With the totality of all that is,
And may be beyond!

The physical
Being is tested in myriad
Ways in the imperfect world

While the
Awakened one keeps
Ascending to their
Metaphysical source

That's the
Significance of every
Human soul

Who   keeps
Spinning into the grand
Sphere of dreams, ambitions,
Rhythms, melodies; looking
For the elusive truth..."

Copyright © 2023 by J.J. Bhatt

Moral Journey

Truth is
Where clarity is
Supreme

Existence
Is best when
"Self-endeavor is
The prime mission"

Life's but
A silent connectivity
With eternity when
Am an egoless being

My core
Essence is simply
"Self-realization," and

That I wish be
My ultimate moral
Journey at every
Turning point

As I keep rolling
From known to the
Unknown…

Copyright © 2023 by J.J. Bhatt

That's Freedom

When
Human is the locus
Of social and political
Order to be realized

It's essential,
He be the positive
Force in the chess game;
Making a civilized world

When
Humanity keeps
Suffering big time,
It's time, he must take
Responsibility to defeat
The deadly storm called,
"The Seven sin"

When
Humans stand before
An unknown future,
It's essential,
They're fearless
And self-confident
To be
The winners in that
Set chess game!

Copyright © 2023 by J.J. Bhatt

Critique of Life

Explorers
Must arrive at a
Meaningful turning
Point of their quest

For every
Explorer must demand,
A priori knowing of the
Complex reality itself

Let him
Be critic of all
That is symbolized:
God, myths, religions and
So on

Let him
Take on the challenge,
"The typological trials
Errors" of the conceptual
Existence

Let him
Arrive at a right conclusion,
"What is his genuine identity at
Every new beginning for sure..."

Copyright © 2023 by J.J. Bhatt

Being &
Reality

Who knows?
We may be the only
Illuminators of hope
And happiness in this
Lonely Universe

Who knows?
We may be the only
Inheritors of our divine
Destiny in its pure
Essence

In other words,
"Let us be free
From the fear of
Uncertainty and death"

Let us
Dare dance in
This complex web
Called, "All that is"

And keep
Ascending toward
The mystical beauty of,
"Who we are and what we
Ought to be…"

Copyright © 2023 by J.J. Bhatt

Cause & Consequence

It's the
Art that brings
Ever beauty and
Truth; awakening
Every Soul

It's
The love
Between two
Young hearts;
Purifies their
Dream

Its life
That offers freedom;
From ignorance leading
To be the
Illuminating mind

It's the
Continued good
Dialogues; facilitating
Understanding and trust…

Copyright © 2023 by J.J. Bhatt

Eternal Principle

The Vedic
Sears boldly declared,
"*Rit* is the moral code that
Operates independent of
Any external agency neither
Divine nor whatever."

Dharma is the
Consequence calling for
Moral duty of humans to
Defend good against evil

In other words,
It's the *Karma* or the personal
Responsibility of every human;
Ensuring stability, peace and
Harmony in the world

That in brief is
The universal, but pragmatic
Vedic wisdom a´ la the
"Sanatan Dharma in action."

Copyright © 2023 by J.J. Bhatt

Hyper-reality

What if,
We're caught between
The real and the virtual
Realities of today

Will it
Change our perception,
"Who we're and where
We're heading?"

Is today,
A fast comingling of
Humans and their
Techno gimmicks or
What?

What if,
We're already being
Silently manipulated
By the smart thinking
Machines or not?

Wonder,
Where will it all ends?
I mean, what will be
Fate of human freedom
While being in this
Human form!

Copyright © 2023 by J.J. Bhatt

Song of Soul

"I,"
What a
Paradoxical
Existence that's
In conflict with his
Core essence

Indeed,"I" is the
Metaphysical mystical
Mystery; being born and
Reborn in the palm of
Eternity

"I' what an
Effloresce Bliss,"
Albeit an Anthrocosmic
Connectivity; seeking
His truth

So now
You know,
"Who is " I,"

Yap,
Just you're moral
Voice guiding toward
"All possibilities you
Own."

Copyright © 2023 by J.J. Bhatt

Being &
Eternity

Time
Passes, and as
The set journey
Nears its death

In such a
Moving complexity,
Only the
Awakened souls
Ensures this
Magnifique universe

Indeed,
In such an evolving
Reality,
All seems symbolic
Expressions of the
Being & eternity
Into uncertainty,
"All that is…"

Copyright © 2023 by J.J. Bhatt

Footprints

Human,
Always a reflection
From the cosmic
Mirror

Indeed, a
Holographic image;
Evolving through
Myriad wonders
And riddles

Again,
Human alone is
Compelled to be the
Hero of his time

For he alone
Must face his truth
While his adventure is
On

Human,
What a continuum
Historic experience;
Defining
The very essence at
Every turning point of
His birth…

Copyright © 2023 by J.J. Bhatt

Caveat

When
Lovers fail to
Understand,
They fail
In many ways

Often they
Fail being unable in
Sustaining fidelity

For love,
Is a serious
Moral responsibility

Of course,
Between two lovers;
Taking sacred vows

Oh yes,
'Love is sweet, but a
Very fragile human
Feeling."

Watch out,
Love may be
Soul soother, but
A Sharpe dagger as well!

Copyright © 2023 by J.J. Bhatt

Eternal Light

Only through
"Prolonged
Dialogues," seems

Possible to
Arrive at the gate
Of Truth

Only through
Clarity, we can
Own
An indomitable
Will to win

Our
Understanding,
Compassion and
Dignity leading us to
"Enlightenment"

Life is a
Mystical journey.
It's a
Collective venture.
That's the very core
Essence to exist…

Copyright © 2023 by J.J. Bhatt

Being
Forever

Each born
Is a moving saga of
Ethical judgment

Each born
Is the cosmic glow
Passing

Through the
Light and the dark
Mystical experience

Each born;
Seeking internal
Harmony at every
Turning page
Of the story

Each born
Is the panoramic
Vision to know,
His/her "Self-Truth,"
Only…

Copyright © 2023 by J.J. Bhatt

Logical Necessity

"I," the
Undefined Being,
Who's a fascinating
Soul evolving through
Life after life

"I" always a
Wondering world
Loaded with million
Unknowns yet to be
Resolved

"I," the
Objectification of
Many riddles yet to
Arrive at a definite
Conclusion

"I" of course,
A logical necessity
To clarify, dignify
And to move the moral
Compass to the "North."

Copyright © 2023 by J.J. Bhatt

JAGDISH J. BHATT, PhD

Brings 45 years of academic experience including a post-doctorate research scientist at Stanford University, CA. His total career publications: scientific, educational and literary is nearly100 including 60 books.

Made in the USA
Columbia, SC
26 September 2023

23233996R00085